If You Walk
Down This Road

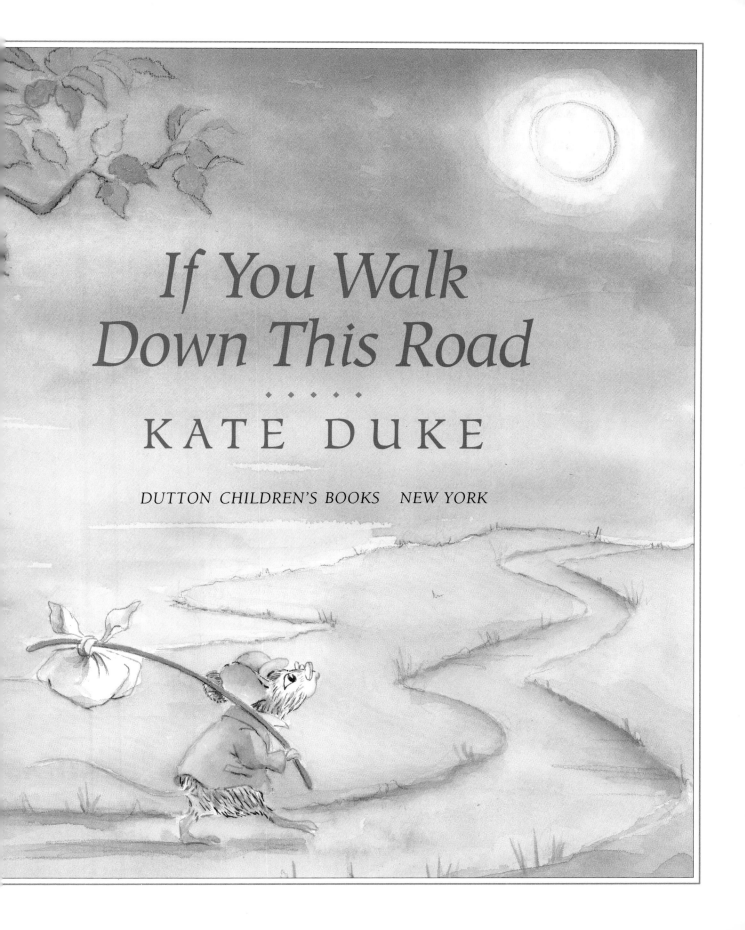

If You Walk Down This Road

KATE DUKE

DUTTON CHILDREN'S BOOKS   NEW YORK

Library of Congress Cataloging-in-Publication Data
Duke, Kate.
If you walk down this road/Kate Duke.—1st ed.
p.   cm.
Summary: Lizard's log, Fox's den, and other animal homes
are discovered on a walk down the road.
ISBN 0-525-45072-6
[1. Animals—Habitations—Fiction.]   I. Title.
PZ7.D886If   1993
[E]—dc20   92-27685   CIP   AC

Published in the United States 1993 by
Dutton Children's Books,
a division of Penguin Books USA Inc.
375 Hudson Street, New York, New York 10014
Designed by Riki Levinson

Printed in Hong Kong by South China Printing Co.
First edition   10 9 8 7 6 5 4 3 2 1

To Sidney

If you walk down this road,
you will come to a town.

The name of the town is Shady Green.
Who lives here in Shady Green?
Come a little closer and you will see.

Who lives here at the top of a hill?

Grandmommy Cottontail lives on the hill.

Who lives here in a moss green log?

The whole Lizard family lives in the log.

Who has a house with a view of the sky?

Old Brown Owl has a view of the sky.

Who lives here in a dark, dirty den?

Rascally Fox has a smelly old den
where he likes to entertain his sly red friends.

Who has a house full of silver and gold?

Vain Lady Jay loves her silver and gold.

Who lives here in the tree next door?

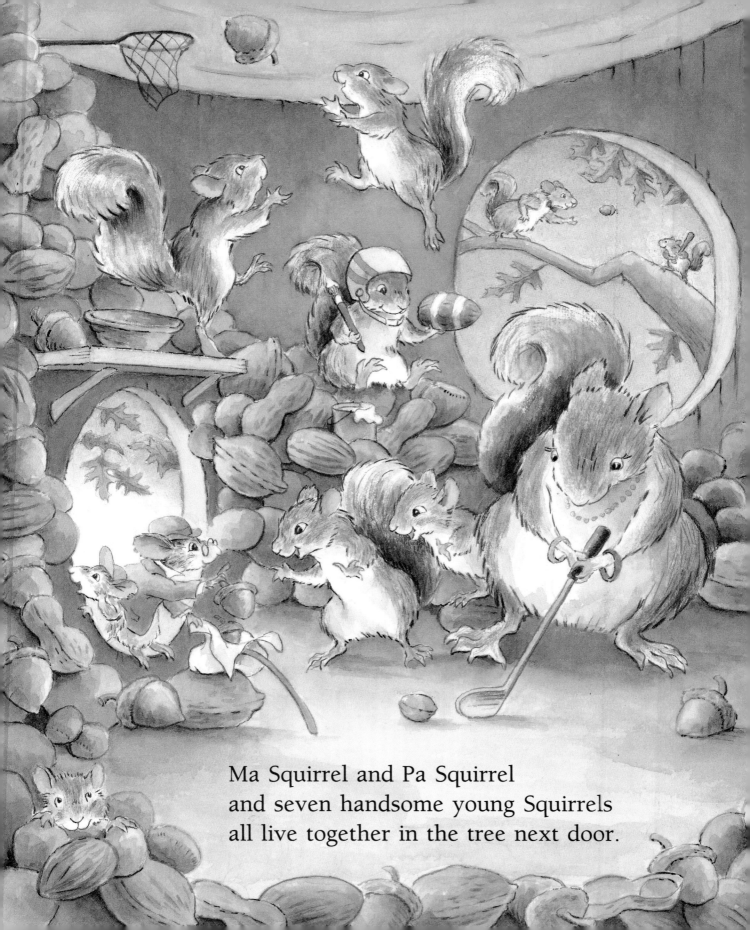

Ma Squirrel and Pa Squirrel
and seven handsome young Squirrels
all live together in the tree next door.

Who built a house in the middle of a stream?

The clever Beaver sisters chopped branches and trees
and built a snug house in the middle of the stream.

Who lives here among the pickerelweeds?

Dragonflies live among the pickerelweeds.

Who lives alone at the end of a hole?

Shy, blind Mole lives alone in his hole.

Who lives here at the far end of town?

Nobody lives here, no one at all.

Someone's moving in, though.
Everyone in Shady Green is coming
down the road to help.

Who is going to live
in this brand-new home?

A brand-new neighbor
has come to Shady Green.